orphic

orphic

Klara Coku

iUniverse®

ORPHIC

iUniverse books may be ordered through booksellers or by contacting:

iUniverse
1663 Liberty Drive
Bloomington, IN 47403
www.iuniverse.com
1-800-Authors (1-800-288-4677)

Because of the dynamic nature of the Internet, any web addresses or links contained in this book may have changed since publication and may no longer be valid. The views expressed in this work are solely those of the author and do not necessarily reflect the views of the publisher, and the publisher hereby disclaims any responsibility for them.

Any people depicted in stock imagery provided by Thinkstock are models, and such images are being used for illustrative purposes only. Certain stock imagery © Thinkstock.

ISBN: 978-1-4917-9021-2 (sc)
ISBN: 978-1-4917-9022-9 (e)

Library of Congress Control Number: 2016902762

Print information available on the last page.

iUniverse rev. date: 02/18/2016

The American Dream was no easy task to take on, and yet, you dropped everything to travel to this brand new world only to ensure us three would have a shot at a bright future and we could never thank you enough; truthfully, I don't think we would even know how. You left everything behind and for that, we are forever in your debt.

So thank you, Mom and Dad, for your courage, your wisdom, your strength, your dedication and your love. Thank you for always believing in me, pushing me to chase my dreams and teaching me that giving up just simply isn't an option.

Alda and Klaudio, you guys gave me an unofficial career a long time ago, peacemaker. Who knew out of the three of us, you two would be the ones to both choose the same architect route when you can hardly agree on what color the sky is. Thank you guys, for always having my back and accepting me for the black sheep that I am. I am proud to be your sister.

To my Uncle Edi, our foundation, who fearlessly paved the way for the rest of us, providing us with everything we needed to get on our feet in this country, and more; without you, we are nothing. To my Uncle Tini, who always made sure to keep us laughing until our stomachs hurt, even during our hardest and lowest moments; without you, we wouldn't know pure laughter. To my Aunt Vida, who never failed to successfully feed a packed house of three families day after day with your incredible home cooked meals, and for always sneaking me an extra scoop of ice cream. To my Aunt Bratila, who in a matter of months went from a mother of one at the time, to a mother of seven.

Knowing I will always have my big crazy Albanian family to fall back on has always been my motivation to be myself, dream, achieve.

This is for all of you.

Love always,
Klara

"Follow me, as I transform poison into poetry" - k.c.

ORPHIC

Klara Coku

Cover design and illustrations by: Klaudio Coku

sometimes,
the pain we tolerate
is more profound
than the pleasure that awaits
when we decide to let go

I tried to tell myself that none of it was my fault
that the bad choices I made in life
were a product of the bad hand I was dealt
but I knew better
I knew exactly was I was doing

The Devil was driving
but I was the one giving the directions
and all I could do
was hope we wouldn't crash

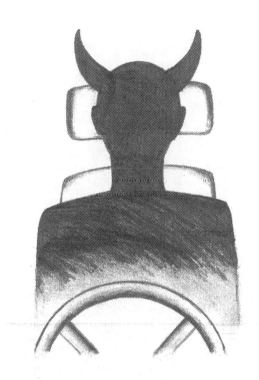

Maybe I invested too much time
into people who didn't appreciate it
and not enough time on myself
and maybe I did too much
for people who deserved so little
and not enough for myself
and maybe I had a habit of
helping others first
knowing I needed the most help
and maybe that's why
I deteriorated
and maybe that's why
I lost myself

Being your friend was the hardest thing I've ever had to go through. It was exhausting, sitting there with our group of friends having to pretend like you're just one of them, when I wanted nothing more than for everyone else to disappear, to walk up to you, look into your eyes and tell you how much I wanted you, all of you. How I wanted to explore your body, your taste, your touch, your mind, your deepest secrets, your thoughts, your aspirations, your biggest fears, your ambitions. I wanted to tell you how I dream about you sometimes, how you're the last thing I see when I close my eyes and the first thought that comes to my mind when I open them.

But our friends never magically disappeared, and you never saw me as any more than just one of them.

and when that day comes
and you're sitting on your porch
smoking a cigarette
while sipping on your glass of whiskey
you'll wonder what it would've been like
to have her sitting there by your side
but just like your cigarette now only ash
and your whiskey now nothing but an empty glass
you'll realize that she too was merely a product of your harmful consumption

bad for you,
but goddamn she was addicting.

I was trying to tell them I was losing, but nobody listened. Now, they pathetically replay my old voicemails, re-read texts I sent them, sometimes they'll even binge watch my favorite show, or play my music in the car as they spend the entire ride reminiscing their favorite moments with me. It always ended the same, in tears.

I always wondered though, which one of them cried because they were sad, and whose tears were mixed with guilt.

Empty bottles mask the living room floor
but the pain lingers,
I need something more.
Ah! Yes, there's the white powder I was looking for.
Straight line, fade out, repeat.
Straight line, fade out, repeat.
On my way to see you again,
only you knew how to get me back on my feet.
I'm trying hard not to lose my grip
as I carry your favorite white rose.
Wait, no, I don't think I can do this,
note to self: next time, higher dose.
Well, here we are again, I made it
here to give you another piece of me,
what're you waiting for?
Take it!
The rain is blending with my tears,
I should go now,
It's getting late.
I'll be back tomorrow with another piece of me for you to take.
I'll see you at midnight darling, alright?
The graveyard is always the most peaceful that time of night.

she said "I don't do this often"
as I pushed her back against the wall
but her experienced hands gave away her lying mouth.

I had prepared myself for the damage I was about to do.
I watched your eyes fill with tears, and felt your heart fill with hatred as you received the words that had formed in my mouth.

What I didn't prepare for, however, was the retaliation you had planned.

The ground is too cold for you baby, and you always were afraid of the dark.

I'm so sorry.

He said
I can't say I ever loved her, no.
I was simply fascinated by her darkness.
So fascinated in fact, that I let it consume me
and before I knew it, she was illuminating brightness,
while I was so engulfed by the dark,
I wasn't sure if I could ever find my way out.

Such a shame, I thought—
he made the ultimate sacrifice for love,
and he didn't even realize it.

The lights are all off and
the town is quiet as I lay in bed listening to the crickets chirping
while I patiently wait.
All of a sudden, car lights flicker outside;
twice fast, then once more.
Our signal.
It's time.
I open my window and quietly climb out.

I hop in the car as we drive off into the night.
The place is packed, I knew off the bat it was going to be a good night.
He grabs my arm and leads me to the dance floor where it reeks of marijuana
and spilled alcohol, but I didn't mind it. We danced, we smoked, we hooked
up, we drank, we got high and before sunrise, he dropped me off and I
climbed back in the same way I left. I fell asleep almost instantly because I
was tired and needed the rest.

I had church in the morning.

Saturday sinner.
Sunday saint.

You know, they say
morals don't exist
and a rule is simply an illusion
and sure
breaking the rules will get you places
but what about the staring faces?
You can only get so far
before reality kicks in,
then do you still win?
You see, society has invisible lines,
lines meant not to be crossed,
because once you do,
you'll get tossed.
Tossed into the pile of
wannabes and rejects,
lowlifes and regrets.

I wanted to help
but he picked up the shattered pieces by himself.
Why won't he let me help?
I tried to hug him
but he won't move a muscle.
Frozen, staring into space.
He was just like snow in December;
beautiful, but cold.
I tried to wipe away his tears
but falling they remained,
another piece of my heart shattering with every drop.
Hopeless.
Him. Me. The world.
Shattered love, dreams, future.

Flatline,
as I follow the angels home.

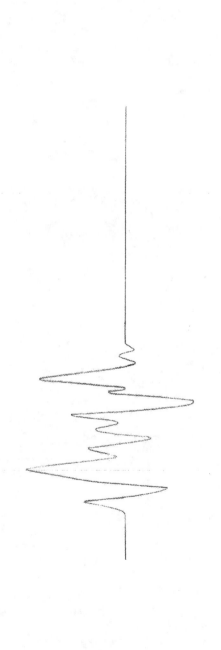

I understand losing someone
to a car accident
cancer
suicide
a heart attack
those are losses out of your control
but losing yourself?
that's a sin sweetheart
and the struggle to find you again?
that's your hell

we tend to overcompensate for love lost
we find ourselves doing more
trusting more
believing more
loving more
sacrificing more
putting our all into the next one
leaving pieces of ourselves behind

and then we wonder why we're all lost

crying for no reason
putting on an act
having to bottle your feelings
believing no one cares
pain
falling asleep with tears in your eyes
carrying tissues around just in case
drastically losing weight day by day
losing your grip on the world
feeling worthless
no longer having interest in anything
getting lower grades in school
being alone
lying in bed wishing the pain would go away
turning plans down with your friends to avoid seeing them
repeating "I'm fine" over and over
looking in the mirror and hating the monster looking back
not letting anyone in
not seeing a way out
wondering why God put you on earth in the first place
smiling only in your dreams
not seeing a future
not having hopes and dreams, only nightmares
self-inflicting pain
cutting deep enough to hurt, but not enough to kill
asking why you
not knowing why you're depressed
wondering if that fall would do the trick
hoping pills will numb the pain
realizing you don't belong
deciding your own unfortunate fate
knowing your end is near and being perfectly okay with it
writing a good bye note
pulling the trigger and not being afraid

and they said I was too young to know depression.

Klara Coku

She was the kind of girl who let herself suffer
in the hopes of allowing him to correct his mistakes,
over and over, again and again.
With every chance she gave him,
a piece of her sanity went along with it.
He didn't love her,
he didn't know what love was,
his level of emotion not able to fathom such complex, yet simple idea.

Tears turned to smiles with fake promises,
smiles turned to tears with broken promises.
His sweet words nothing short of fireworks;
beautiful to witness, dangerous to be touched by.

Sanity and patience
wearing thin,
time and air
running out.

Please don't love me,
because I have yet to learn how to love myself,
and until I do, I will destroy the both of us,
and that's not fair to you.

Be careful around people who say things like
"he died" instead of "he passed away"
"she fucked up" instead of "she made a mistake"
"you look terrible" instead of "are you okay?"

because here's the thing about those people,
just like you, they too are aware of the alternatives,

and that's the scariest part.

We live in a society where we are our own worst enemy, our own harshest critic, our own creator of fear, our own destroyer of strength. We are the weak generation, the generation that won't be mentioned in history books, because we're the generation that didn't care to make a difference, to have our voices be heard, engrave our name in future minds.

We are the fallen, but by no means, did we fall heroically.

As I am driving to New York
I pass Ground Zero
and my eyes begin to water.
The road is no longer visible.
 "Ok class, take out your math books," says Ms. D.
Two students start arguing
"Hey, watch where you're going."
I turn my head and notice the angry driver driving alongside me.
I had almost rammed him over.
"How did you ever get your license?"
I turn my head back to the road.
Tick, tock, tick, tock.
Math class would be over at 9:00
The time goes by slowly.
At about 8:58, Ms. Robyn rushes into our room,
she calls to my teacher.
"Please, step outside with me for a second."
I hit the breaks as I notice a big truck turning into a street.
My eyes are still teary and I can barely see,
so I dig into my purse and take out a tissue.
"Thanks for the tissue," Ms.D. says to Ms. Robyn,
as they walk back into the room.
We are all wondering what is going on.
Class, please put your books away.
"Why, what happened? What is going on?"
"Are you ok?"
"I'm fine."
I answer the cop who pulled me over for running a red light.
He gives me a ticket and leaves.
I roll my window back up and continue driving.
My eyes get puffier from crying.
"Kids, something terrible has happened, the Twin Towers have been hit."
The class is quiet.
We didn't know what to do or say.
"You are all getting dismissed, so one by one, you all have to call home."
My turn finally came.
"Hi, Daddy."
"Hi Sweetie, where are you?"

I'm in New York, don't you remember I told you I was going today?"
"Oh yes, I forgot," he says.
"But your curfew is still midnight."
"Yeah, yeah I know. I love you,"
I say and hang up the phone.
"On the phone with us just moments ago was the Mayor of New York,"
says the news anchor.
"What has just happened is unbelievable, the Twin Towers have been hit."
I'm in my bed, crying, scared, terrified.
This was too much for a 5th grader to handle.
I get up to grab a snack, and go back to my room.
NBC was doing a special on 9/1.
The news anchor says,
"Today marks the 14 year anniversary of 9/11/200."
I glance over at my calendar;
Friday, September 11, 2015
My eyes fill with tears once again.
Turning off the T.V.,
I drift into sleep.

She couldn't stand the kind of music I listened to. She used to say rock was an unnecessary genre. Sometimes, when I would play it in the car, I would glance over and I would watch her face scrunch up in annoyance and I would laugh, and she would roll her eyes.
But then one day, she stopped scrunching her face at my music,
not even a flinch.

That was when I felt it,
the end, it was near.
and then just like that,
she was gone.

and I never listened to rock music again.

Shots went off over his head. He was young and innocent, he didn't deserve this. Often times, he would ask God for some protection, but God never answered.

He was cuddled in the corner of his room praying for this nightmare to be over. The room was small; a bed in the far right corner, an old wooden dresser next to the bed, on top of it laid a Bible, one that he read from every night. He glanced over at the Bible, wishing he could walk across the room to reach it but was too afraid to get up. As he waited in the dark for the streets to quiet down, images of his father popped into his head. The little boy was only seven when his father lost his battle with cancer, but the images were vivid. Since his dad died, he always thought of him as his guardian angel. Always by his side, guiding him, whenever he needed him. Reminiscing of those days when his dad was around helped keep the little boy calm until the streets were finally quiet.

He got the courage to go outside and look for his family. Living through a war was like living through hell, but worse, because he was alive and breathing …and alone. The streets were covered in blood, lifeless bodies were spread throughout. He looked around, scared, lost, angry, and confused. He spotted two men moving in the shadows. Their large bodies resembled that of a huge bear. They started making their way toward him, raising their weapons, as if protecting themselves from this harmless little boy. He froze with fear. Stopping in front of him, the taller, more built one asks,

"What's your name?" he was still holding his weapon firmly across his chest in the upright position.

"Dominic" the trembling little boy replied.

The two men looked at each other for a moment. They weren't sure what to do with the boy. Do they let him go? Do they ruthlessly kill him like they did so many others?

Of course they kill him, what made him any more special than the other hundred plus lives they had taken. With one quick nod toward each other, the tall one raises his weapon and points it downward, directly toward Dominic's forehead. Dominic stood there. Arms by his side, eyes wide open, displaying the greatest level of fear. Never one to put God second, Dominic started silently praying.

All of a sudden, breaking away from his current state of shock, disbelief, and prayer, Dominic looks up in amazement. Hope now took over the fear displayed in his eyes only a few seconds ago. Another figure emerges from the shadows. The familiar looking figure, ever so gracefully, glides over, stopping next to Dominic, right by his side. The two men look at each other in confusion. The figure's left hand slightly rests on Dominic's shoulder. The touch sends an electric shock throughout his tiny, fragile body. At the same time, a sense of relief swept over him.

The men were confused, not sure what Dominic was staring at or why he suddenly looked more relaxed, but as if following some unspoken directions by a higher authority, the men looked at each other, and quickly walked away, still holding their weapons, but gradually lowering them as they disappeared into the night.

where are all these bad people
if we all claim to be so good?

the liars
the "haters"
the fakes
the lowlifes
the cheaters
the intolerable

where are they?

they're inside us
we are all those things
we are the bad people
we warn our friends about

And unless you've walked off that airplane clutching your moms hand, looking around with tears in your eyes at this world that was now supposedly your new home, you will never know what the life of a foreigner is like. You will never know how trying to learn a new language was a personal challenge and a public struggle, how trying to fit in at school was a daily failure. You will never fully comprehend how we envied the way you sat down at lunch and laughed at stupid things with your friends — we wanted to laugh too, but instead, we cried. We cried a lot. We cried when we got bullied, we cried when we got lost, we cried when we didn't understand, we cried when we saw our parents cry, but eventually, we dried our tears, put on our brave faces, and joined in on the laughter, because laughter is universal after all, we just needed to hear ours out loud for the first time.

One day, you'll look back and reflect on your actions
and you'll have to come to terms with them.
One day, my favorite song will come on the radio
and it'll be my voice ringing in your ears.
One day, you'll catch a whiff of my perfume walking down the street
and it'll knock you senseless.
One day, you'll hear the person in front of you at the coffee shop order my
favorite drink
and you'll taste me in your mouth again.
One day, you'll get caught in the rain
and the raindrops will make your vision blurry,
and you'll finally understand
what looking at you through my tear filled eyes was like.

One day, reality will hit you.

Hard.

I wish we took the time to see
all the kids living in poverty.
Who am I to just ignore
all those suffering because they're poor?
Who am I to just walk by
as these children ask themselves why;
why they never had a home
why they're growing up alone
why they never have enough food
why people walking in the street are so rude.

All the racism and the hate,
all of which we helped create.
Does it matter who's black or white?
Does it matter who's wrong or right?
We should be helping our nation stay united,
instead we're helping it become divided.

night after night
no matter how many tears her pillow tasted
how many screams her blanket muffled
how many failed attempts on her life the walls concealed
she never let anyone in on the misery
because morning after morning
the sun would brightly come up and greet her with complete oblivion
and she would greet it back with just as much brightness

I came across an old man today.

He was sitting at the bus stop,

staring at nothing and at everything at the same time.

I sat next to him, pulled my book out and was about to start reading when—

"My wife committed suicide Thursday."

whoa

"I'm really—"

"Don't say sorry, Son. Don't say you're sorry."

okay

"The note said 'I hate who you turned me into. I hate who I've become. I hate God for letting you cross my path, but most of all, I hate us.'"

holy shit

"I had a rose, Son. A beautiful rose. But the whole time, I only paid attention to the thorns."

goddamn

"She may be 6ft. under, but I'm the one paying the ultimate price."

wow

"It feels as if the very dirt I threw on her casket multiplies and slowly suffocates me with every flashback I have of hers."

Jesus!

"I'm being buried alive."

He never broke his stare.

I still pray for you, you know?
Even after all this time,
I still pray for you.
I pray you grow.
I pray you learn.
I pray you repent.
Because life is long,
but I hear payback for sinners is longer.

And I swear to this day he still thinks leaving had everything to do with him— it didn't. I needed to find myself first before I allowed myself to get lost in him. But life isn't fair, and time waits for no one, because he eventually found somebody who was willing to get lost in him without fear, and that's who we're all looking for at the end of the day, isn't it?

Stooping to her level would've been easy, almost too easy, you know? She was one of those people that never looked at her own actions, never inconvenienced herself to help those that mattered the most, always did the right things for the wrong people. She never seemed to understand that nobody else appreciated her efforts and attention and how much I craved it. It was fascinating I must say, watching her disregard my existence completely and yet, I never thought of doing the same to her, not even for a second. I couldn't turn my back on her when she needed me, be selfish, hurt her. I wanted to, God, how I wanted to; but I couldn't stoop that low. Besides, you know what they say; there's no risk of a traffic jam on the high road.

Nothing will fill you with more emptiness
than when you realize
you have exhausted all your options; there is nothing more you can do.

Now, you can either let that feeling consume your entire being
and slowly eat you alive, or you can take it as a sign from God.
Believe that this is His way of telling you He will take it from here.

It will all be okay now.

was i the one?
he asked
who dimmed the sparkle in her eye?
who made those crystal blues cry?
he wondered if one day
karma will make him pay for what he's done
but then he realized
karma had already won
because he may have hurt her
whenever he had the chance
but as she walked away
she killed him
with her final glance

Klara Coku

how lucky are we
to have complete control
over everything
you don't like the shirt you're wearing?
change it.
you got a bad grade?
study harder.
hate your job?
quit.
missing someone?
call them.
annoyed by someone?
dump them.
need an escape?
read.
smoke a blunt.
drink until your blood turns to alcohol.
drink until it feels like your heart is pumping Vodka.
love a song?
replay it.
replay it until the lyrics become a part of you.
replay it until the beat matches you footsteps.
replay it until it no longer makes you happy.
replay it until it makes you sad.
replay it until you hate it.
just do whatever you need to do
because you only get one shot
at this thing called life
please, don't let it go to waste.

why is that, you think
that our generation is so unlike every other
how did we become so fucked up
we need alcohol to numb our pain
social media to feel accepted
sex to feel wanted
drugs to escape reality
but is this reality that cruel?
or is it the only side we choose to see
why?
because we need the attention
the sympathy
the feeling of entitlement;
entitled to roll one, pass it along and let the smoke carry our sorrows away
because we are the downhearted
desponded
depressed generation
and we like it.

i neglected you right when you needed me the most
i heard you but i didn't listen
i looked at you but i didn't see
i didn't just watch you slowly succumb to your wounds
i handed you the knife

i understand if you can't forgive me
i have yet to forgive myself

if your plan was to hurt me all along
you should've left before you made me cry
because I only shed tears when someone dies
and I cried for you
which means now,
now you're dead in my eyes.

he hurt the one who loved him
she loved the one who hurt her
neither of them saw anything wrong with their actions

I would often catch him staring at me, and whenever I would look back at him, he never looked away, he would just stare longer, harder. It almost felt like he was trying to communicate with his eyes what his mouth couldn't bear to say, except we didn't have that connection; I don't think we ever did. You know the connection I'm talking about, those couples you see nod at each other and you just know right away that an understanding took place, or you see a small curl form on the side of their lips and you realize an inside joke was just mentally laid out. I envied those couples, they seemed so at peace with themselves, with each other. With us, everything felt forced, like we were trying so hard to knowing we were only fooling ourselves. I often wondered if we would ever find our peace, but until then, we sat and stared until one of us eventually broke the stare first.

She put every once of energy she had left into bettering herself. She picked up and reassembled all the broken pieces he left behind, which proved to be no easy task. You see, he didn't only break her physically, that part was easy to repair, those bruises faded, the scars healed, the wounds were neatly hidden behind Band-aids, but rather, it was the mental damage she had trouble with. She was never the same after him.

They said she was found hanging from her closet.

And him? Well, he made it.

They always do.

but sometimes,
forever is shorter than we think
stars are dimmer than they appear
promises hold less truth than we believe
people are weaker than they seem
and you…
you are the coldest winter night
the deadliest cancer
the smoke cloud of a fatal last cigarette drag
the bullet lodged inside a dying soldier
the antagonist in my worst nightmare
the unfortunate fate of my reality

Her demeanor didn't match her personality. On the outside she was the Ice Queen, but on the inside, her heart was a raging fire, wanting nothing more than to find somebody who could see past the tough exterior, but her walls were built so high she forgot what the other side looked like.

Klara Coku

Not everyone is going to appreciate your flame,
some people prefer the ashes
and that's okay,
but promise me
they won't be the reason you burn out.

Even on the coldest, most brutal December night
I still have to crack my window open at 3am
because it's around that time
thoughts of you suffocate me the most
and I can't breathe
and it never gets easier

Klara Coku

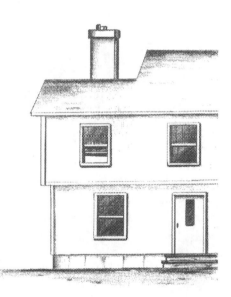

I'm sorry I didn't try harder, I wanted to, I swear I did. Maybe I had forgotten how, maybe you stopped giving me reasons, or maybe my excuses got better with time. Or maybe my love for you ran out and I couldn't bring myself to tell you, so I dragged us on. It wasn't fair to you, I get it now. I remember you putting your all into my happiness, you let it consume you, doing everything in your power to see my smile at least once a day, but then your efforts turned into seeing me smile once a week, then once a month. Then, one day, you stopped caring too, and I was relieved, because I wasn't sure how many more smiles I could fake, and I'm sorry.

whoever said time heals all wounds
obviously never felt the tip of your knife before

She reminded him of the most perfectly wrapped present under the tree; only a matter of time until it was ripped to shreds.

and Christmas always was his favorite holiday.

I remember the day
I promised you I would never hurt you.
Please forgive me, Darling.
We all lie, don't we?

she was too lethal to want
but I couldn't help myself
giving into the desire
I pulled her in close
and as our lips collapsed
she breathed fire down my throat
her tongue acid in my mouth
and I was more than willing to burn

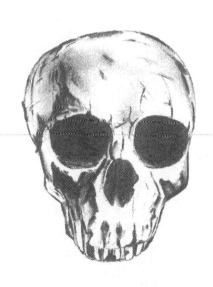

We ran out of love
because we consumed it all
to fulfill our love
for hurting each other.

Klara Coku

he wasn't
what she was used to
he wasn't
like the rest of them
he wasn't
fascinated by her beauty
mesmerized by her eyes
captivated by her body
no
he challenged her
tested her
questioned her celebrity
and it drove her insane
and she hated it
and she loved it
and she hated him
and she loved him

Where is everyone? Why don't they try to stop her from committing this permanent solution to all her temporary problems? Her thoughts are racing. Sitting on the counter rests a gun, fully loaded and suddenly, her fragile hands reach for it; for death. No one knows the emptiness she feels, or the pain she endures. Those who left the emptiness behind are gone, those who inflicted the pain don't care.

A single shot is fired, finally relieving her of anymore suffering, now in the hands of God. They loved to see her lose, but who won?

The pearly white atmosphere is almost blinding. She looks around, asking herself if this is Heaven. Her question was answered when an angel appeared and without a word, the angel motioned to follow him and so she did without giving it a second thought, because she wasn't scared anymore, she felt safer than ever. The angel led her to God waiting for her standing in front of a beautiful gate.

"My Dear, you have disappointed me. You know this isn't the answer."

She is confused, staring, speechless. She never believed in God before so why was He talking to her? How? She failed to understand that God gave her life and she intentionally took it away.

"I am willing to give you another chance, my child, a chance to start over, a chance to prove to me you are willing to work through your problems."

She was at a loss. She looked over at the angel who gave her a reassuring smile, followed by a nod.

It was dark now, and she was back in a familiar room. She looks down at her hands and realizes she is holding a gun. She gently sets in on the counter, feeling His presence as she slowly walks away.

The day I put myself in my unborn daughters' shoes,
was the day I decided to walk away from him.

Only when I met him did I realize
that reaching the bottom of the bottle
was not the only way to get drunk.

Twenty-four.

In one night, that was a new record, but no surprise, she was his best girl after all. She was only 13 when he found her, all alone sitting down on the cold, hard concrete between Lexington and 59th. He didn't even go out that night looking for new "peaches" as he liked to call them, but there she was. He sat down next to her, but she didn't even acknowledge him, prompting a mental challenge he automatically created in his head, which of course, he had to win.

"A little too young to be out here all alone, aren't you? Your parents know where you are?"

Nothing.

"Are you cold? Here, take my jacket." he offered.

She docsn't flinch as he puts his jacket around her shoulders.

"Thank you." she whispered so low that her visible breath in the cold air was the only indication she even spoke at all.

Perfect. He knew he couldn't let this one slip. In his twisted mind, it felt like she was practically begging him to help her.

That night, she opened up to him right there on that concrete, told him how her dad left when she was 8 years old, how her mom was an abusive drunk and drug addict who brought home a different man every week, how almost every one of them raped her and her mom never did anything about it because alcohol was more important than her own child, how her little brother's death two years ago was ruled accidental, but she witnessed her drunk mother push him down the steps with her own two eyes.

If only those walls could talk.

Flash forward six years and about 2190 prayers later, one for every single day since she met him. As soon as she had gotten to the apartment that night, she realized she had made a mistake, but it was too late. She officially belonged to him and there was no way out. His grasp on her, mentally and physically, was too strong for her to break free from.

But tonight, she got through 24, that was a new low, even for him. It was 4am, and she could hardly keep her eyes open.

"Get up, go take a shower you look filthy, your next is about to come in and I will lose him if I present him to you looking like that," he hissed.
She got up, showered, and sat in bed, waiting.
But 25 never showed.

"Must've made up with his wife." she thought to herself as she let out a chuckle and drifted off to sleep.

She woke up to a metal bar from the bed frame crushing her skull as he repeatedly struck her. She rolled off the bed onto the floor where he then got on top of her and raped her, over and over and over, until she "learned her lesson to never fall asleep while waiting for a customer who was simply running late."

She started praying. It was really working this time, her crushed skull didn't hurt anymore, she felt less and less pain. Then, everything went black.

And finally, she was free.

It was about four years after the breakup that I ran into her.

"Do you remember that one stormy night, we fell asleep on the porch at your house because you had forgotten your keys and everyone was asleep?"

Yeah.

"The way you held me that night, like you were shielding me from all the evil in the world, was the night I knew."

Knew what?

"That you were going to be my favorite victim."

I have slammed the door on peace,
but held it open for chaos,
because you only taught me how to start the war,
but you never showed me how to win it.

We risked everything for
a glance from afar,
a hug at the bar,
a kiss in the car.
She was both my kryptonite and my morphine,
and I knew it wasn't fair to the ring on her finger,
and she knew it wasn't fair to the man in her bed and yet;
I continued to love her,
and she continued to allow it,
teaching me every single day the difference
between being with her, and being hers;
and I kept showing up to every lesson.

It was draining, I'll tell you that much.

He had a way of terrorizing me with words that would anger the Gods, but a touch to calm the storm that even the angels couldn't master.

The day of the wedding
was the last day I saw her.
Every day after that,
I saw us.

"I hate you!" was the last thing I said over the phone right before I hung up on him.

We had never had a fight as bad as that one and to be honest with you, I can't even remember what it was about. Probably something stupid and I overreacted, as usual. He was so calm on the phone that October night, not saying much, letting me get my anger out like he normally did. After about 15 minutes of me screaming on the phone, he finally said "Okay, baby. Please, let's drop this okay? I will call you as soon as I get home and we can talk about it some more. I love you, Mel." But I wasn't having it. I said "I hate you!" and I hung up.

He would call me Mel sometimes, short for melodramatic, which I would whine to him about how much I hated the nickname, but deep down, I don't think it ever bothered me as much. I guess I knew I did tend to blow things out of proportion at times, I just never thought one day, I would be paying the ultimate price for it.

By the time I got to the scene that night, they had already taken his body away, all that was left was his car wrapped around the tree. They told me he died on impact so at least I knew he didn't feel any pain. The police recovered his cell phone at the scene, which they assumed was what caused the crash.

"Hate, baby girl, is simply confused love. Talk to u later, I love—"

He never got to hit send.

It was a warm November night, three years since the last time I had seen her.
We were driving around, 3:30 in the morning with no destination in mind,
alcohol had replaced the blood in our veins.
Out of nowhere she says "My lucky number is seven, did you know that?"
I did.
I knew everything about her.
How much she was terrified of dogs,
how she hated riding in the backseat,
how her biggest fear was suffocating to death
because she was claustrophobic.
How she loved to be in control
but deep down,
she didn't mind someone else taking over once in a while.
How she acted tough,
but around me that wall would break at times,
or maybe I was the only one to see through it.
I wasn't sure.
What I did know, was that even years later,
she was still the only girl
who could make me
laugh,
cry,
do stupid shit with no regrets,
no matter how reckless.
The only girl,
I still gave a fuck about.

We pull into a gas station,
the clock on the wall reads 4:03am
and as the cashier is handing me my change,
I can't help but notice his name tag.
"Hi, my name is Seven"

I look over, she's glancing at it too,
half a smile spread across her face
and that was the crazy thing about her, you know.
She had this insane ability
to make you feel like
nothing made sense
and everything made sense
at the same goddamn time.

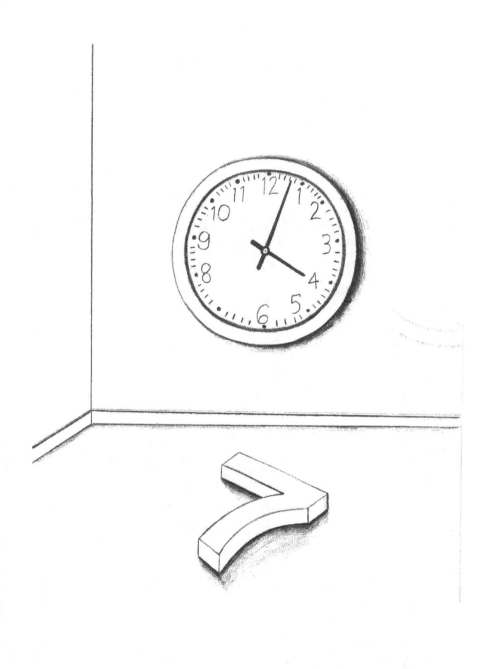

but when she asked
if he saw them still together in sixty years
he didn't look at her
he looked directly through her
and that's how she knew
she just didn't belong there anymore.

I think the last time I had peace of mind
was thirty seconds prior to you walking into my life
and since then
it has been mayhem and confusion
lustful and passionate
disruption and commotion
sensual and everlasting

a beautiful chaos, if you will.

he was the reason behind my smile
but he never got to see it
as it spread across my face
while I walked away

It was simple; we loved,
and when we thought we could love no more,
we just loved harder.

Remember in elementary school when your teacher would tell you to share, making it clear the toys weren't yours? You never wanted to though, and it was yours as far as you were concerned, but at the end of the day, you still put it back because in the back of your mind, you knew it didn't belong to you...

Well, that's what being with her was a lot like.
She never truly belonged to me,
and I knew it was only a matter of time
until I had to put her back.

Sometimes,
just sometimes,
it's okay to give up.
Not everything was meant to be achieved,
not everything was meant to be within your reach.
Don't ever let them make you feel like you're a failure
for not seeing something all the way through.
Some things just weren't meant for you, and that's okay.

Klara Coku

...in fact,
he was a little too good to be true
and it was then that she realized
she had finally found someone she could hurt first.

only after I lost you did I realize
you'd been throwing sugar at my open wounds
instead of salt like everyone else

My hand always gets a little shaky
when my pen is about to write your name.

Klara Coku

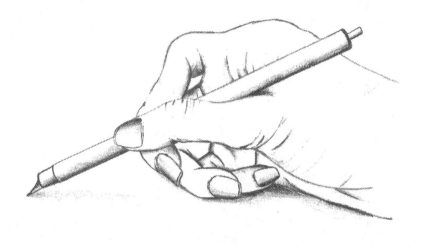

i tasted your next attack in my mouth
i felt it curl on your lips
and i knew this one would be bad

bad
but not lethal
because the pain was familiar now
i felt empty without it
and only you knew how to deliver
and i always made sure to say thank you

as I lay in the dark,
I feel his stone cold hands press against my crawling skin
his breath engulfs my face like flames
I am consumed by hatred
for him, yes
but mostly for me
for not being able to scream
for not being powerful enough to strangle the evil out of him
with my bare hands
rid him of this demon that has washed over him
my rock
my best friend
my protector of innocence
the very one stripping me of that
with every stroke
every whisper
every moan

The war in my head started over trying to forget you
and ended when I realized
that it was your scent I was inhaling every time I breathed her in
your sparkle I saw
every time I looked into her eyes
your voice I heard every time she moaned my name.
I was fighting a battle I knew I had already lost
but this war in my head kept you alive
so I didn't mind.

I fear you.

I fear one day you will look at me and decide that is the last time you want to see me, that you will touch me and decide that is the last time you want to know what I feel like, that you will hug me and decide that is the last time you want to hold me, that you will kiss me and decide that is the last time you want your lips on mine.

I have an irrational fear of you, and I'm not sure how to overcome it.

Death by a thousand paper cuts was how he worded it. I knew because I heard him talking every night by my bedside, talking to God, talking to me. The doctors told him I was in a coma, that I couldn't hear, couldn't feel, but he knew. I wanted so badly to talk back, tell him he can leave, move on with his life, tell him this wasn't fair to him, that just because I'm in pain doesn't mean he has to be as well. But I couldn't speak, the tubes in my nose hurt, the needle in my vain taped to my hand stung, my eyes burned, aching for me to open them, but I didn't have the strength. Please God, let me open my eyes, just so I can look into his, but alas, it did not seem like this was happening anytime soon; today marks one year here. I knew this because he made sure to tell me the date every single day since the accident. That was he how started every morning, it was what kept me alive, knowing that when he woke up, his voice was the first thing I heard. Visitation hours clearly didn't apply to him, and the staff was well aware, they stopped asking him to leave after the first week, realizing he wasn't going anywhere. He would tell me stories, take me back to happier times, he never dwelled on the bad. Sometimes, I wished he would though, I wish he would talk about the accident, take me back, but he never discussed it and it made me so angry. I was entitled to know what happened to me! The last thing I remember was coming face to face with a truck and his hand flying across my chest, a reflex he had every time he slammed the breaks a little too hard. This time though, it was clear his arm couldn't help me.

Wait, what's happening, why does the doctor sound so panicked? I feel fine, at peace actually. Why is there so much beeping? It's so loud! Baby, please tell them to stop the beeping, it's hurting my ears.

I can see his face now, oh my God, I can see his face again. It's so beautiful, despite his dark circles from all the sleepless nights, and his puffy eyes from all the crying, he is so perfect. But he doesn't seem so happy to see me, I'm confused.

"Baby, it's me, I'm up, I'm here, I love you," I whisper as I stroke his face, but he doesn't even flinch.

"Good morning, Sunshine. Today is January 9th. Until we meet again."

you gave me life
but then

changes

you watched me die
slowly

I would forgive you,
but I've lost all control
of my emotions

Klara Coku

Don't ever accept an apology,
if changed behavior doesn't follow.
Saying sorry is easy,
showing sorry is vigorous.

and when they were together
it was as if the whole world stopped
paused
so they may feel everything to the fullest extent
and gravity's only purpose
if merely for that very second
was to push their bodies toward each other
but then
reality
and all of a sudden
the world was in motion again
as were they
walking away from each other
knowing they could never be
should never be

it was just better this way

I would be lying if I said I didn't shed a tear, but it didn't hit me right away. I started to feel her absence slowly. I no longer found strands of her golden blonde hair all over the house, and eventually, the lingering smell of her perfume slowly faded away. Sometimes, I would be listening to music and her favorite song would come on and I'd catch myself about to say "your favorite part is coming up." Little by little, I started to feel the sting of not hearing her voice over the phone when she would call me to complain about the little things; about somebody taking her parking spot at work, or how her boss was being a jerk because she was three minutes late to work, or how the guy at the hot dog stand didn't line up the mustard and ketchup on her hot dog the way she liked it. I missed her kissing my collarbone; she said it was her weakness. That was when I shed my first tear, when I realized I would never stop feeling her absence. It almost felt as if life before her never existed.

we went from making love to having sex
wanting to tolerating
making conversation to making small talk
dinners together to "I'm not hungry."
off beat lip-syncing car rides to blasting music hoping it'll drown out the silence
holding hands to hardly walking in sync

we deteriorated as beautifully as we had loved;
slowly, and then all at once.

Being with somebody I loved who didn't love me back was brutal. It was as if I saw the world in color, and she was limited to black and white vision, and every time I talked about how beautiful something was, she looked at me like I was crazy.

Maybe I was.

But if you must cry beautiful
let me cry with you
let me help you close your wounds
by reopening mine
because the only way to last forever
is to be broken together

I closed many doors in my life,
but I always made sure to leave yours cracked open.

Promise me, that when you look back on us
you won't hate yourself for pushing me away.
I already have enough hate in my heart for the both of us.

I wasn't supposed to let anybody in
I made sure my heart was sealed
and yet, you somehow managed to get through
I don't know how, but you did

And for that, I thank you.
You saved me.

all of a sudden,
I found myself smiling only when he was around
finding comfort only when he held me
finding peace only when he kissed me
finding myself only when he looked at me
it was unlike anything I'd ever experienced
and I never wanted it to end.

Instead of promising to never hurt each other,
let's do the opposite; promise me you'll be my biggest heartbreak and I'll do the same,
so that when it does eventually happen, we can at least say we saw it coming.

I struggled to put into words how I felt about him,
everything came out so generic, cliché.
He was caring, kind, gentle, loving, affectionate, devoted.
Yes, but he was so much more than that.
It was all the little things he did. How he knew how to make my coffee in the morning just the way I liked it, sometimes even better than I made my own, how he never minded when I stretched my legs across his lap when he drove, how he would look directly at me when taking a picture and never at the camera because "no lens could ever capture what's right in front of him."

We had our bad days, absolutely, but even on our worst day, no matter where he was, what he was doing, he would call me at exactly 6:12pm. You see, 6:12 represented June 12th, the first time he laid eyes on me and he made sure to I never forgot how much that day had changed his life; to this day, I struggled to make him understand how much he changed mine.

He was rare. He was raw. He saved me.

By the time I realized
he didn't come into my life to save me
but rather simply love me
it was too late anyway
he was gone
and once again, I was alone
and it's your fault
you left me so damaged
that I no longer look for lovers
I look for saviors

We were the modern day version of Shakespeare's most coveted screenplay. Fully aware of the risks we took being together, we did it anyway; unable to determine which one of us cared less about the consequences. She was Juliet, I couldn't stay away, her touch gave me chills, her kiss gave me peace. My hands fit perfectly in the arch of her back, making it impossible for me to let go.

But I was Romeo,
and we all know how the story ends.

I kept going back to him, looking for happiness exactly where I lost it.

It took me so long to realize that what I was doing wasn't okay, it wasn't normal.

He wasn't normal.

Normal people did not go around killing the souls of others at their convenience.

It wasn't your big smile
or the way your eyes danced full of life.
No.
It was the way my heart skips a beat
every time my name rolls off your tongue.
The way you grab my hand
starting from the forearm
caressing your way down to my fingertips
sending chills down my spine
with every electric movement.
The way you stand on your toes
to reach my lips.
The noise you make in my mouth
when I lift you up.
The way I can feel your lips form a brief smile
as they rest on mine.
The way you get excited about things like
the sound of a bird chirping
a child laughing
an elderly couple holding hands
a full moon
the first snowfall.
The way you take comfort in the rain.
The way you can't stay mad for longer than five minutes
because that's five minutes too long to waste being mad.
The way you listen.
How you ease my pain; one hand on my shoulder, the other on my cheek.
The way you love me.
The way I need you.

When will loving ourselves become socially acceptable again?
When will glamorizing unrealistic images of beauty
become the kid nobody wants to hang out with?
In a world full of self hatred, loathing, competition, judgement, indifference,
be the voice of self love, acceptance, peace, admiration, adoration.

I never really knew how to reply to "What's your biggest fear?" In general, people expect an answer like spiders, heights, or clowns, but all those things were so trivial to me. What's my biggest fear? My biggest fear is not learning how to cope, taking the easy way out, never amounting to anything, failure, misery. I fear going back to that dark place, handful of pills on one hand, note in the other. I fear seeing my moms face in my nightmares, the face I saw when she found me on the bathroom floor fighting for my life. I fear the color white because it was the only thing I saw flashing in front of my eyes right before they revived me. I fear my lack of self control, I fear the thoughts in my head.

So, what's my biggest fear?

Me.

I am my own biggest fear.

Klara Coku

I'm not quite sure when it was that you lost yourself, but I guess it doesn't matter, does it? Because wherever you've gone, I see it's too late for you to return and so with that, I too, must leave.

and I'm so sorry, but I can't wait around forever and I'm afraid I will lose myself in my quest to find you, and to be quite honest, I'm not sure you even want to be found anymore.

I feel my existence diminish before my very eyes
my screams outlast my last breath
as I try unsuccessfully to make peace with my soul
just one last time

Klara Coku

I hope one day you wake up
and realize it could be worse.
I hope when you're getting ready to take your last breath,
you think of the tragedy that was me.
I hope I give you strength.
I hope I inspire you
to breathe, to live, to love, to last.

My time is up and I thank you for yours.
Be well.

Yours faithfully,

Klara Coku

Contact Klara
Instagram: instagram.com/klarac91
Email: klaracoku@hotmail.com